Anonymous

Edwin, the Young Rabbit Fancier

And other Stories

Anonymous

Edwin, the Young Rabbit Fancier
And other Stories

ISBN/EAN: 9783744750684

Printed in Europe, USA, Canada, Australia, Japan

Cover: Foto ©Andreas Hilbeck / pixelio.de

More available books at **www.hansebooks.com**

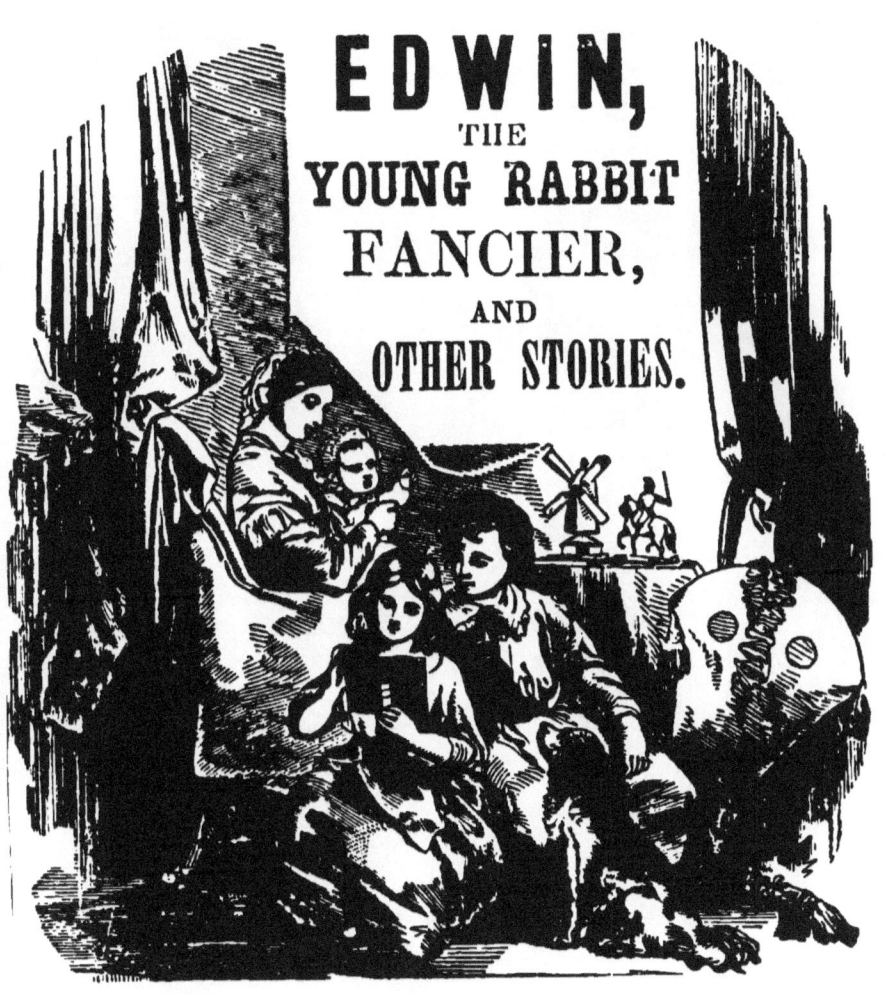

EDWIN,
THE
YOUNG RABBIT
FANCIER,
AND
OTHER STORIES.

BOSTON:
CROSBY & AINSWORTH,
NEW YORK: OLIVER S. FELT.
1866.

STORIES.

EDWIN, THE YOUNG RABBIT FAN-CIER.

DWIN was a very tender-hearted boy, and very eager about a thing when he took it into his head; but his enthusiasm very often left him just at the time it ought to have remained with him. Thus he never pursued any study or amusement for any length of time with profit to himself, and often fell into very grievous errors.

"Oh! dear mama," said he one day to his mother. "I do so much wish that I had something for a pet; there is Charles Jones has a sweet little bird, and cousin James has a squirrel. I should so like something for a pet Do, mama, buy me something—a Guinea pig, or a couple of pigeons, or a rabbit. Oh! I saw such a beautiful white rabbit yesterday.

"Ay, my dear," said his mama, "I am afraid you would soon grow tired of your rabbit, as you did of your gun, and bow and arrow, and ship, and rocking-horse."

"Oh! but a rabbit is quite different, mama; you can love a rabbit, you know, and coax it, and feed it, and make it happy. I should go out early in the morning, and pick some nice clover for it, and some thistle, and dandelion, and marsh mallows. I know how to feed rabbits—I have learned all about it. I must not give them too much green stuff, but some nice bran and oats; and then I could make a little trough for it to eat from, you know; and—and—"

"I am sure, my dear, it would be too much trouble to you; rabbits require a great deal of care and attention, and you so soon get tired of any thing you take up, that I fear it would soon suffer from neglect."

"I am sure I should never *neglect* it, mama; and if you will give me a shilling, I can buy a beauty—a real white French rabbit, with red eyes, and a coat like swansdown. Do, mama, give me a shilling."

"No, my dear," said she, "I really must refuse you."

Now, although Edwin was a little boy, he said to himself, "I know it is only because mama wished to save her money; 'tis not because she really thinks I shall neglect the rabbit, but because she does not like to part with her money." He thought himself very cunning? did he not?

So Edwin began to pout and whine, and to tease his mama, being determined to let her have no peace. "You know, mama," said he, "I shall be so fond of it; I will make it a house, and then I could cut down some grass, and dry it, and make hay for it to lie upon; and I could sow some oats for it in my garden; I should not want any thing else to amuse me all the year round."

Whether to humor Edwin or to teach him a lesson, I will not say, but his mama gave him a shilling, and off he ran, and purchased the milk-white, red-eyed rabbit he had so longed for.

Joyful enough was he when he brought it home; he paraded it round the house, showed it to every member of the family, housemaid, laundrymaid, footman, and cook, and every body praised the rabbit, as the most beautiful creature they had ever seen.

The next morning Edwin rose by times, and began to look for wood to build his rabbit house. He procured saw, nails, and hammer; and at last found some old planks, and began to saw them, and cut them, and chisel and plane, till his little arms ached again.

He had soon cut two or three pieces of board up, but to no purpose; one was too short, another too long, a third had a knot in it, and a fourth was spoiled in splitting. Vexed with his want of success, Edwin said, "I shall not make him a house to-night—he must be contented with being fastened in the coal-hole to-night, where he will have room plenty."

So bunny was put into the coal-hole, with a handful of cabbage-leaves, and told to make himself happy till morning, and as it happened to be election night, Edward went to amuse himself by making bonfires."

In the morning Edwin went to the coal-hole to look after bunny. There it was sure enough, but, instead of its being a beautiful white rabbit—hy hopping about among the coals—it had become almost as black as the coals themselves.

"Well, I never!" said the little boy— "what a dirty little thing it is, and so he tried to catch it; but bunny not liking to be caught, led the youngster a fine dance in the coal-hole, and at last he fell over a large lump of coal, and dirtied his clean frill and white pinafore.

It was difficult to say which was the dirtiest of the two, Edwin or the rabbit. The little boy, however, being quite out of patience, made no further effort, but shut the coal-hole door, and in great terror ran to the nursery-maid to put him into cleaner trim. He did not go again into the place where the rabbit was that day, and so the poor thing was kept without food, for Edward totally forgot that he had not fed his pet.

However, the next day he again repaired to the place, and having caught bunny, took it into the stable-yard, and put it into an unoccupied pig-sty. The first intention of making a house was

quite given up, and Edwin began to think his rabbit was a great plague; he, however, gave it some more cabbage leaves, and left it.

The fact was, Edwin was getting tired of his rabbit; he, however, bought it a few oats, and gave it a little hay. He went out for a few mornings and gathered a little clover, but in less than a week this was thought to be a great deal of trouble; besides which, the rabbit seemed lame, and did not look so pretty as it did at first.

At last Edwin quite forgot his rabbit for two days, and when he went to look at it he was quite surprised to find it lying on its side. He called, bunny, bunny. The poor thing looked at him, and seemed pleased to see him, for its long ears moved as if it was.

Edwin took it up; it seemed to have lost the use of its hind legs; it squeaked when it was touched; and so the little boy laid it down again. He felt it all over—it was very thin, and seemed half starved.

Edwin now ran and got a saucer full of oats, and placed it beside the poor thing; he also ran to the next field, and plucked some nice sow thistle, and gave it to eat. Bunny looked grateful, and tried to eat, but could not.

Edwin, in placing his hand down by its side, felt the beatings of its heart; it went beat, beat, beat — throb, throb, throb, quicker than a watch; and every now and then its head twitched, and the skin of its jaw drew up, as if it were in great pain.

And yet the poor animal seemed glad to have some one by its side, and rubbed its nose against Edwin's hand; and then it panted again, and its eyes grew dim; it was dying; Edwin now began to cry.

"Oh! my poor dear, dear, dear, bunny," said he, "what shall I do to make you well?—oh! what would I give? Oh! I have killed you, for I know I have. Oh! my poor, dear bunny—let me kiss you, dear bunny—Here the little fellow stooped down to kiss the rabbit. Just at that moment it gave a struggle—in the next it was dead.

Edwin's eyes were full of tears, and when he could see through them, and found out what had happened, he broke out into loud sobs and cries, till he roused the whole house. "Oh! my dear rabbit —oh! I have killed my rabbit—oh! what shall I do?" he uttered, in deepest grief.

"Ay," said his mama, who was called

to the spot by his outcries, " I feared it would be thus:—who would think a house-bred rabbit could live in a damp pig-sty? The poor thing has been destroyed by neglect."

"Oh, yes, dear mama, do not scold me; I know I have been very naughty. Oh, I do love my dear rabbit; I love it more now it is dead than I did when it was alive; but is it really dead, mama! no, is it? it is quite warm, and may get well again,—say it will, there's a dear, dear mother," and then he cried again.

The rabbit was, however, dead; and had caught its death in the way Edwin's mama supposed, by being ill fed and kept in a damp place, by thoughtless, if not cruel, *neglect.*

2

Edwin was overcome with grief,—but it was now too late, sad was that night to him, for something told him that he had been cruel to that he had promised to love. He got no sleep; and early in the morning he arose, and went to the place where his pet was laid.

He wept all the next day; and, in the evening, he dug a grave in his own little garden, close by the side of a young rose tree. Then he wrapped the body in some nice hay, and laid it in its narrow cell, and placed rose leaves upon it, and covered it gently with the earth; and his heart was like to burst when he heaped the mound upon it,—and he was forced to pause in his task by the full gushing of his tears.

"My child," said his mama, who watched him at his sorrowful task, "if you had taken half the trouble for bunny, when alive, as you do now he is dead, he would have been alive now."

"Yes, yes, dear mama,—I know—I know; but do tell me, pray do—will not rabbits go to heaven? Is there not some place where they can be happy? I hope my poor bunny may!" and here the little fellow sobbed again.

"Give me a kiss, my dear boy," said his mama; come leave this spot: and so she gently led him away from the rabbit's grave.

JULIA MARTIN.

N many of the little coves and bays on the coast of Cornwall, small villages may be found—the dwellings of fishermen, their wives, and families. Here, perhaps, they have lived

(20)

THE FISHERMEN.

22

from the time they were born, without a thought or a wish, as far as the land is concerned, beyond the narrow place in which they dwell. The sea is the great object of their cares, for it contains the means by which they live. By the fish which they catch in it, they are provided with meat, drink, and lodging: and too often is the sea their grave. The poor men lead a hard and anxious life in their fishing pursuits; and are often tempted to risk their lives, rather than give up a chance, when a favorable shoal of fish may be expected. The women mostly spend their time in making and mending nets, and drying and salting the fish. Even the children may be always found employed about fish in some way or other.

The very young make playthings of the bones; those about ten or eleven assist their mothers in curing fish; and all, both old and young, feed, with a relish never lost, on the finny tribe. It is a pretty sight, on a fine sunny day, to see the seine, or net, drawn in on the white pebbly beach: it contains, perhaps, many hundreds of fishes, tinted with all the colors of the rainbow. The various families to whom the net belongs crowd down to the shore for their share of the fish; for, as the net costs a great deal of money, the price is divided, perhaps, between half a dozen owners. During the winter season, should there have been any failure in the fishing, great hardships are sometimes felt by these poor people.

TLe stock of salt fish is done; potatoes are dear, and money to buy bread is but scarce. The patience and self-denial shown under such privations is truly to be admired, and might furnish a useful lesson to those whom it had pleased God to provide, at all seasons, with every thing that can make life pleasant; and who are too apt to complain if some of the lesser means of their enjoyment are cut off by a hard winter season.

Rosecreay, one of the fishing villages we have been describing, was. fortunate, during a very severe winter, in having near it a very charitable lady, who had taken a house which for many years had been without an inmate.

Why she remained in a cold and bleak

spot, so far from London, from whence
she came, her friends often wondered;
and her daughter Julia, when she heard
the wind coming in great gusts up the
valley, or the rain beating against the
windows, as if it insisted on coming in,
would wish she was back again in the
pretty house at Kensington. Mrs. Martin was not poor, but she was not rich,
and she had taken the old house for
three years, because the rent was very
low; her own house in town she had let,
and the change was made that her only
son, Frederic, might study as a painter.
How many mothers thus deny themselves
comforts, that they may save money for
those dearer to them than their own lives!
How few meet with any reward for their

self-denial! Mrs. Martin was constant
in her visits to the families of the fishermen; gave them tracts to read; made
clothes for the poor children; and was
always ready, in time of illness, with
medicine for the sick, and soup for those
getting better. She also tried to teach
them cleaner habits; but in this she
failed. Julia soon got tired of going with
her mother to see people who persisted
in having such bad smells in and about
their houses, wondering, at the same
time, that, with water so near, the village was not kept cleaner; to which an
old woman would sometimes reply, that
fish never smell ill to them. One stormy
day in January, Mrs. Martin and Julia
sat at the window watching the huge

waves that came tumbling in, with, as
Julia said, "great white caps on their
heads." The fine weather of yesterday,
said Mrs. Martin, I hear, has tempted
poor John Penman to go out fishing, in
spite of his having hardly got rid of the
fever he has so long had. I am afraid
that as he knew that Frederic is coming
we should like some fish to-day. The
weather changed so suddenly in the night,
that I feel quite anxious lest he should
have been lost. Mrs. Martin's fears were
too well founded, for John Penman, his
eldest son, and another lad, never saw
their homes again: the boat had been
lost during the heavy gale, and all on
board had perished.

How dreadful! said Julia. I wish w•

did not live where we were always hearing and seeing such disagreeable things. We must not, my dear Julia, said her mother, indulge in such selfish feelings; let us rather think what we can do for the poor widow and her or, hans, whether it is disagreeable or not. The next morning, though it was still stormy, Mrs. Martin set out for the cottage of Mrs. Penman; and as Julia thought it was too cold to venture out, she was spared the sad scene that was seen by Mrs. Martin. The children were crying round the bed of their poor mother, where she lay in too much grief to attend to the kindness of the neighbors, who crowded round trying to comfort her.

The room was small and dirty, with

but little furniture in it; but strange to
say, on one side of it hung an old circu-
lar painting, and though it was nearly
black with smoke, Mrs. Martin could see
it was no common picture. With the.
hope that it might prove of some use to
the poor woman, she got the eldest boy
to carry it to her house, sending back by
him a basket laden with food for his
desolate home. Frederic had arrived in
due time the night before, and his mother
now begged him to look at the old painting. Although he had not long been an
artist, he at once saw that it had been
painted by a skilful hand. While clean-
ing it from the smoke and dirt, they
found the name of the painter and of the
lady on the canvas. On inquiry, they

also found that John Penman's father had saved the picture from a great house, which had been burnt to the ground many years ago. Mrs. Martin wrote to the family to whom the painting had once belonged, and they were glad to pay the poor woman, to her great surprise and joy, a handsome sum of money for it. She was then able to buy a share in a net, which her husband had always been too poor to do, and by it was enabled to bring up her family in the humble way to which they had always been accustomed.

Ah! mother, said Julia, what good you have been able to do from always thinking of other people rather than yourself. I will never grumble again at the smells of the fishing village, but try, if I can, to be as useful there as you have been; and Julia, in spite of the cold and bleak winter, well kept her promise.

SUMMER

THE HAYMAKERS.

THE HAYMAKERS.

THE haymakers are working blithely, tossing about the grass, and talking and laughing right merrily. This is a holiday, both for old and young. Many who are employed in manufactures, with their wives and children, obtain leave to work in the fields when hands are scarce; and doing so seems like a new life to them. You may see at the further end, hillocks of grass thrown up in long rows; the haymakers call them wind-cocks; they are piled light and high, that the wind may blow

(35)

through them; but in this part of the field people are tossing the hay about. Gray-headed old men are here, aged women, and children, seemingly without number. Their parents are hard at work and very glad are they to put the "wee things" in safe keeping among the old folks, who yet can help a little. Look at those girls and boys at play—see how they pelt one another with the hay, and roll each other over upon the grass— these are happy days. See those youngsters, scarcely able to totter, how they tumble on the sweet, fresh grass; while those who have strength to handle the rake mimic the labors of their parents, and draw tiny loads along the greensward. Meanwhile the hay is thrown about, and with each returning day comes the same pleasant labor, till the creaking of a wagon, lumbering up the hollow-road from the old farm-house, half way down the hill, gives the signal, which tells that the haymaking season is about to close. A short time elapses, and the creak of the heavy laden wagon is heard ringing over the stones. It comes up again for another load, then lumbers back to the old farm, where laborers are busily employed in placing the hay upon a strong foundation of wattled boughs. Some tread down the hay; others throw it up from out the wagon; till at length loud huzzas, that wake up all the neighboring echoes, announce that all the hay-stacks are completed.

THE REAPERS.

THE village seems deserted. No children on the green running races with each other, or playing hunt-the-slipper on the smooth turf. No old men resting beneath the manorial tree, sunning themselves, and talking with feeble voices, like the aged men of Troy, compared by Homer to grasshoppers; neither is there the sound of the spinning-wheel by the open cottage door, with its rustic porch and clustering hops. All are away to the harvest-field. Let us go there, too. We are all bidden guests at Farmer

(38)

AUTUMN

THE REAPERS.

Drayton's, and our holiday will pass merrily among the reapers.

"Good morning, Goody! Where are you going with your troop of rosy children, all glee and gossip?" "To the harvest-field, young masters. 'Tis a pleasant time, that comes but once a year, and we make the most of it. My master was out before the sun, reaping in the field beside the river; but I had to dress the children and get his dinner, and that makes me late." "Good day, then; we will not hinder you." Away she goes, half running, the children out of breath with delight. They have turned into Johnson's field. Let us follow them. There they are with twenty or thirty others, gathering the scattered ears, as

Ruth gathered them on the plains of
Bethlehem. Look at Goody! How di-
ligently she is picking up the ears! The
children, too, are all helping. Before the
season is over, they will collect at least
three clear bushels of wheat; and if the
weather prove showery, and the wagon
is hurried to the barn, they will obtain
a larger quantity.

Farmer Johnson is at the farthest end,
watching his reapers. He looks pleased,
and with reason, for the rustling corn
stands thick, and the men work cheer-
fully. The Lord of the Field, (for such
the chief reaper is called,) heads the long
line of farming servants. When he
clasps the opposite ears in his strong
arms, they clasp theirs also; when he

thrusts his sickle, they do the same; and there is presently laid low a wide extent of grain, with its garniture of flowers,— the corn-cockle, and scarlet-poppy, sweet basil, and marjoram, herbs Robert and Christopher, Cicily and William—names by which old simplers commemorated worth or friendship, or the villagers of other days associated with the memory of benefactors, whose skill and kindness might be shadowed forth in the qualities of their favorite plants. It seems as if those who bind up the sheaves have some pleasant or grateful thoughts connected with the prostrate flower, for a few are carefully taken from among the rest and put aside.

Before the young wheat springs up,

we shall hear, I fancy, the church-bells ringing merrily, for there are John Gray and Susan Bell hard at work. He has just pulled the prickly stems of the woolly thistle from the corn she is about to bind. Farmer Johnson often tells the men and women to mind their work; but he takes no notice of John and Susan, though many a kindly word passes between them, for he knows that more industrious and well-conducted young persons are no where to be found.

THE PARROT.

THE PARROT.

THE deep affections of the breast,
  That Heaven to living things imparts
Are not exclusively possess'd
  By human hearts.

A parrot, from the Spanish Main,
  Full young, and early-caged came o'er,
With bright wings, to the bleak domain.
  Of Mulla's shore.

To spicy groves where he had won
  His plumage of resplendent hue—
His native fruits, and skies, and sun—
  He bade adieu.

For these he changed the smoke of turf,
   A heathery land and misty sky;
And turn'd on rocks and raging surf
   His golden eye.

But, petted, in our climate cold,
   He lived and chatter'd many a day;
Until, with age, from green and gold
   His wings grew gray.

At last, when blind and seeming dumb,
   He scolded, laugh'd, and spoke no more,
A Spanish stranger chanced to come
   To Mulla's shore.

He hail'd the bird in Spanish speech,
   The bird in Spanish speech replied;
Flapt round his cage with joyous screech,
   Dropt down and died.

NEW AND ATTRACTIVE

JUVENILE BOOKS.

BOSTON:

CROSBY & AINSWORTH.

NEW YORK: OLIVER S. FELT.

1866.

Popular Juveniles.

THE FIRESIDE; OR, HINTS ON HOME EDUCATION. By
A. B. Muzzey, author of "The Young Maiden," "The Young Man's Friend," &c.
16mo, cloth, gilt . . . .

MABEL VAUGHAN. By the author of the "Lamplighter." 1 vol. 12mo .

TUNE-BOOK FOR THE CONGREGATION. A Collection of Tunes
for use in Societies, and for Vestry and Conference Meetings. Cloth . . .

THE ECLIPSE OF FAITH; or, a Visit to a Religious Sceptic. By Henry
Rogers, author of "Reason and Faith," and "Miscellaneous." 12mo, cloth .

A DEFENCE OF "THE ECLIPSE OF FAITH." By its Author.
Being a Rejoinder to Prof. Newman's "Reply." Also the "Reply" by Prof. Newman. 1 vol. 12mo, cloth . . . .

THE STARS AND THE EARTH; or, Thoughts upon Space, Time,
and Eternity. 18mo, flex. cloth . . . .

HYPATIA; or, New Foes with an Old Face. By C. M. Kingsley, author of
"Yeast," "Alton Locke," &c. 1 vol. 12mo . . . . . .

THE TEACHER'S ASSISTANT; or, Hints and Methods in School Dis-
cipline and Instruction. By Charles Northend, A.M. 12mo. . . . .

**WARE'S FORMATION OF CHRISTIAN CHARACTER, AND
SEQUEL.** 16mo, bevelled red edges . . . .

**CHANNING'S SELF-CULTURE, AND LECTURES TO THE
LABORING CLASSES.** 16mo, bevelled red edges . . . . .

DEXTER'S SERMONS. Twelve Discourses. By Henry Martin Dexter.
With Portrait. 8vo, cloth . . . .

STREET THOUGHTS. By Rev. H. M. Dexter, Pastor of the Pine-street
Church, Boston. With illustrations by Billings. 16mo, cloth . . . .

HOME COOKERY. A Collection of Tried Receipts, both Foreign and Domes-
tic. By Mrs. J. Chadwick. 12mo, half bound . . . . . .

DUELS AND DUELLING. Alphabetically arranged. With an Historical
Essay. By Lorenzo Sabine. 12mo . . . .

I'VE BEEN THINKING. By A. S. Roe . . . . . .

HOW COULD HE HELP IT? By A. S. Roe . . . . . .

STAR AND CLOUD. By A. S. Roe . . . .

TO LOVE AND TO BE LOVED. By A. S. Roe . . . .

TRUE TO THE LAST. By A. S. Roe . . . . . .

LONG LOOK AHEAD. By A. S. Roe . . . . . .

THE NORTH AMERICAN REVIEW. Issued in numbers quarterly
Per annum . . . .

THE MARRIAGE OFFERING. A Compilation of Prose and Poetry. By A. A. LIVERMORE. With two engravings on steel by Andrews, from designs by Billings. Cloth, gilt . . . .

do.   do.   do.   do.   cloth, extra, gilt. . . . . . .

PASTOR'S WEDDING GIFT. By Rev. WILLIAM M. THAYER, 16mo, muslin, gilt, extra . . . .

TUPPER'S PROVERBIAL PHILOSOPHY. 12mo, muslin . .
do.   do.   do.   muslin, gilt, extra . . . . .
do   do.   do.   morocco, do. . . . . . .

GLEANINGS FROM THE POETS. By Mrs. LOWELL. 12mo, muslin
do.   do.   do.   muslin, gilt, extra . . . . .
do.   do.   do.   morocco do. . . . . . .

OUR FAVORITE POETS. Illustrated with engravings. 1 vol. 12mo, cloth
do.   do.   do.   full gilt . . . .

HISTORY OF THE UNITED STATES. By MURRAY. Illustrated. 1 vol. 8vo, muslin . . . .
do.   do.   do.   do.   sheep . . . .

LIBRARY OF NATURAL HISTORY. By GOULD. 400 engravings. 1 vol. 8vo, muslin . . . .
do.   do.   do.   do.   sheep . . . .

CHRISTIAN BELIEVING AND LIVING. A Series of Discourses by Rev. FREDERICK D. HUNTINGTON, D.D. 12mo . . . . . .

SERMONS FOR THE PEOPLE. By Rev. F. D. HUNTINGTON, D.D. 12mo, cloth . . . .

HOME AND COLLEGE. By Rev. F. D. HUNTINGTON, D.D. 16mo : .

JACK IN THE FORECASTLE. By Capt. JOHN S. SLEEPER. Eight engravings. 12mo, cloth . . . .

LIFE AND RELIGION OF THE HINDOOS. With a Sketch of my Life and Experience. By JOGUTH CHUNDER GANGOOLY. 16mo, cloth .

MARION GRAHAM; or, Higher than Happiness. A Novel. By the author of "Light on the Dark River." Cloth . .. .

RELIGIOUS LECTURES ON THE PECULIAR PHENOMENA IN THE FOUR SEASONS. By EDWARD HITCHCOCK, LL.D. 16 mo, cloth . . . .

THE ADVENTURES OF JAMES CAPEN ADAMS. Illustrated by 12 engravings. 12mo, cloth . . . .

THOUGHTS TO HELP AND TO CHEER. Comprising a Selection from Scripture, a Meditation, and a Poetical Extract for each day in the year. 24mo, blue and gold . . . .

WELL BEGUN IS HALF DONE; AND, THE YOUNG ARTIST. With six fine illustrations printed in oil colors . . . .

WILD SPORTS IN THE FAR WEST. By FREDERICK GERSTAECKER. Illustrated with eight crayon drawings in oil colors. 12mo, gilt, cloth . . .

YOUNG ISLANDERS; or, The School-boy Crusoes. A Tale of the Last Century. By JEFFREYS TAYLOR. Cloth . . . .

Miscellaneous.

ARABIAN NIGHTS' ENTERTAINMENTS. Illustrated, muslin .
  do.   do.   do.   muslin, gilt, extra .
  do.   do.   do.   morocco, do. .

NOBLE DEEDS OF WOMEN. By MISS STARLING. 12mo, muslin .
  do.   do.   do.   do.   muslin, gilt, extra . . . .
  do.   do.   do.   do.   morocco, do. . . . .

BANCROFT'S LIFE OF GEORGE WASHINGTON. With illustrations. 12mo, muslin . . . .
  do.   do.   do.   do   muslin, gilt, extra .

LIFE AND CAMPAIGNS OF NAPOLEON BONAPARTE. With illustrations. 12mo, muslin . . . .
  do.   do.   muslin, gilt, extra . . . . . .

FROST'S LIVES OF THE PRESIDENTS OF THE UNITED STATES. With Portraits. 12mo, muslin . . . . .
  do.   do.   muslin, gilt, extra . . . .

YOUNG LADY'S OFFERING. By Mrs. SIGOURNEY. 12mo, muslin .
  do.   do.   do.   muslin, gilt, extra . . . .
  do.   do.   do.   morocco, do. . . . .

YOUNG MAN'S OFFERING. By Professor ANDREWS. 12mo, muslin .
  do.   do.   do.   muslin, gilt . . . . .
  do.   do.   do.   morocco . . . . .

FLORA'S LEXICON. An Interpretation of Languages of Flowers. Colored illustrations.   muslin . . . . .
  do.   do.   muslin, gilt, extra . . . .
  do.   do.   morocco . . . . .

TALES FROM SHAKSPEARE. By CHARLES LAMB. 12mo, muslin .
  do,   do.   do.   muslin, gilt, extra . . . .
  do.   do.   do.   morocco, do. . . . .

THE YOUNG MAIDEN. By A. B. MUZZEY. With two engravings on steel by Schoff, designed by Billings. 16mo, cloth, gilt . . . .
  do.   do.   do.   cloth, extra, gilt edges . . .

POPULAR TALES. By Madame Guizot. Translated from the French. With six colored engravings . . . .

PETER THE WHALER. By Wm. H. G. Kingston, Esq. Illustrated .

PLAYMATE. A very beautiful book, with nearly 200 engravings. Square 16mo., gilt, cloth . . . .
do.   do.   do.   do.   extra .

ROBINSON CRUSOE. By De Foe. Square 16mo. Illustrated, muslin .

ROBIN HOOD AND HIS MERRY FORESTERS. By Stephen Percy. Illustrated . . . .

ROBIN-NEST STORIES. By Mrs. Madeline Leslie. Illustrated by Billings. Price 25 cents, single volume. Set, six vols.. . . . . .

ROUND THE WORLD. A Tale for Boys. By W. H. G. Kingston. With illustrations. 16mo, cloth, gilt . . . .

SICKNESS AND HEALTH OF THE PEOPLE OF BLEA-BURN. 18mo, gilt, cloth . . . .

SEED-TIME AND HARVEST. By Trauermantel. With six colored illustrations . . . .

STORIES ABOUT THE INSTINCTS OF ANIMALS, THEIR CHARACTERS AND HABITS. By Thomas Bingley. Illustrated .

STORIES AND LEGENDS FROM MANY LANDS. Illustrated . . . .

SWISS FAMILY ROBINSON; or, The Adventures of a Father, Mother, and Four Sons, in a Desert Island. The general progress of the story furnishes a clear illustration of the first principles of Natural History, and many branches of science which most immediately apply to the business of life. Complete . .

STORIES OF THE CANADIAN FOREST; or, Little Mary and her Nurse. By Mrs. Traill (sister of Agnes Strickland). Illustrated . .

SALT WATER; or, The Sea Life and Adventures of Neil D'Arcy, the Midshipman. By Wm. H. G. Kingston, Esq. Illustrated by Anelay . . . .

TALES FROM THE HISTORY OF THE SAXONS. By Emily Taylor. Illustrated . . . .

TITANIA: TALES AND LEGENDS. Six colored illustrations . .

THE WONDERFUL MIRROR. With colored engravings. 16mo, cloth

THE WIND SPIRIT AND THE RAIN GODDESS. With nearly 100 beautiful colored engravings . . . .

TALES WORTH TELLING; or, a Traveller's Adventures by Sea and Land. Illustrated with 133 engravings . . . . . .

WHEN ARE WE HAPPIEST? By the author of "The Boy of Spirit," &c. . . . .

Juvenile Libraries.

EACH IN A NEAT BOX, AND EVERY VOLUME FULLY ILLUSTRATED.

DOG CRUSOE SERIES. By R. M. BALLANTYNE, KINGSTON, BOWMAN, and others. 6 vols. 16mo, cloth . . . .

The Gorilla-hunters.
Audubon.
Round the World.

The Bear-hunters.
Dog Crusoe.
John Chinaman.

SALT-WATER TALES. By WM. H. G. KINGSTON. 4 vols. . . .

The Young Islanders.
Peter the Whaler.

Mark Seaworth.
Salt Water.

MOUNT-VERNON JUVENILES. 6 vols. . . . . . .

Life of Washington.
Love of Country.
Bears of Augustusburg.

Life of Lafayette.
Legends of Brittany.
Hurrah for the Holidays!

MERRY TALES AND STORIES FOR YOUNG FOLKS. 6 vols.

Stories of the Canadian Forest.
Pictures of Comical People.
Canadian Crusoes.

Tales of the Saxons.
The Kangaroo-hunters.
Merry Tales.

THE MOLLY AND KITTY JUVENILES. 6 vols. . . . .

Molly and Kitty.
Children's Trials.
Tales and Legends.

Seedtime and Harvest.
Belle and Lily.
Holly and Mistletoe.

THE LEILA BOOKS. By ANN FRASER TYTLER. 5 vols. . . . . .

Leila at Home.
Leila in England.

Leila; or, The Island.
Mary and Florence.

Mary and Florence at Sixteen.

THE ROBIN-NEST STORIES. By Mrs. MADELINE LESLIE. 6 vols. .

The Robins' Nest.
Little Robins Learning to Fly.
Little Robins' Friends.

Little Robins in the Nest.
Little Robins in Trouble.
Little Robins' Love to one another.

LITTLE FRANKIE STORIES. By Mrs. MADELINE LESLIE. 6 vols. .

Little Frankie and his Mother.
Little Frankie and his Father.
Little Frankie at his Plays.

Little Frankie and his Cousin.
Little Frankie on a Journey.
Little Frankie at School.

TALES AND STORIES WORTH TELLING. 4 vols. . . . .

· Robin Hood.
Mother's True Stories.

Bingley's Instincts of Animals.
Tales Worth Telling.

THE JEWEL CASE. 6 vols. . . . .

The Pearls.
Guizot's Popular Tales.
· Well Begun is Half Done.

Many a Little makes a Mickle.
A Will and a Way.
Nannie's Jewel Case.

EDGEWORTH'S EARLY LESSONS. 5 vols. . . . . . .

Frank.
Sequel to Frank.
Rosamond.
Harry and Lucy.

Harry and Lucy, concluded.

MRS. TUTHILL'S JUVENILE LIBRARY. 14 vols. . . .

I will be a Gentleman.
I will be a Lady.
Happy Days, and the Warning.
A Strike for Freedom.
Onward! Right Onward!
The Sickness and Health of the People of Bleaburn.
The Boarding-school Girl.
The Boy of Spirit.
When are we Happiest?
Hurrah for New England!
The Childhood of Mary Leeson.
Ellen Stanley, and other Stories.
Anything for Sport.
Keeper's Travels in Search of his Master.

YOUNG PEOPLE'S LIBRARY. 12 vols. . . . . .

Alphabet of Birds.
Alphabet of Animals.
Young Rabbit-fancier.
Annie and the Elves.
Stories and Legends.
The Boa Constrictor.
Johnny and Maggie.
The Princess Unca.
Lucy's Canary.
Christmas Eve.
Rose Tremain.
Just in Time.

UNCLE SAM'S LIBRARY FOR THE BOYS AND GIRLS.

The Christmas Eve.
George and his Dog.
Stories and Legends.
The Picture Alphabets.
All for the Best.
The Eskdale Herdboy.

SIX PLEASANT COMPANIONS FOR SPARE HOURS. Embellished with nearly 200 engravings. Square 16mo, fancy cloth, gilt . .

Little Freddy and his Fiddle.
Little Lizzie and the Fairies.
The Road to Fortune.
Saddler Muller's Wendell.
Tony, the Sleepless.
Finikin and his Gold Pippins.

BOUQUETS FOR CHILDREN. Collected by L. MARIA CHILD, MARY HOWITT, and others. 5 vols. . . . .

New Flower for Children.
Flowers for Children.
Arbell's School-days,
The Children's Year.

Berquin's Children's Friend.

YOUTHS' PICTORIAL LIBRARY. With over 500 illustrations. 12 vols., 16mo, paper covers, per set . . . .
do. do. muslin, gilt, do. . . . .

Poems for Little Folks.
Tales of the Great and Brave.
Stories of Animals.
Christmas Stories.
Stories of Natural History.
Rabbit's Bride, and other Stories.
Tales of Adventure.
Stories of Foreign Countries.
Casper's Adventure.
Fairy Stories.
Fables in Verse.
History of Birds.